# When Dog Grows Up

By Lucille Hammond
Illustrated by Eugenie

A Golden Book • New York
Western Publishing Company, Inc., Racine, Wisconsin 53404

One morning Dog looked in the mirror, but all he could see was the top of his head.

"Someday," said Dog to himself, "I'll be a much bigger dog. Someday, I'll be all grown up." And he began to think about what he would like to be when he grew up. "How will I ever decide?" he said.

Dog went over and stood by the
window. Outside, a police car hurried by.

"That's it!" thought Dog. "I'll be a police officer with a siren in my car, and I'll chase robbers down the street."

Dog liked the idea of driving very fast. Well, then, he would be a race car driver! His car would almost fly through the air as it went around the track, and everyone would cheer when he came in first.

"But why couldn't I *really* fly through the air? I could be an astronaut!" Dog thought.

Dog kept on thinking. He picked up his book of fairy tales and looked at the pictures. He wished that he could have been a king, just like the one in his favorite story. He imagined living in a castle with a high tower on the top.

"It would be fun to draw the pictures that go in books," thought Dog. If he were an illustrator, he could make colorful pictures for beautiful books. He'd draw other dogs, birds, buildings, bridges—everything.

Then Dog decided it might be more exciting to *build* bridges than to draw them. He would work with other clever dogs and build a bridge over a wide river.

Dog went back to the mirror. He
jumped up and caught a glimpse of his
face. But he almost knocked over his
mother's favorite vase.

He had another idea. Instead of building new things, he would have a repair shop and put all sorts of broken things back together.

Rather than a repair shop, Dog thought he might prefer a toy store. He'd have to play with all the toys so he could tell his customers which ones were the best.

"It would be so much fun, though, to play the drums in a big city orchestra!" Dog thought.

Dog liked the city, but he also liked the country. Maybe he'd be a farmer and grow his favorite foods. His chickens would lay delicious eggs.

Thinking about food made Dog hungry. He was glad when his mother called, "Time for lunch!" Dog stopped thinking about being grown up. For now he was a hungry young dog, and that was enough.

"Coming!" answered Dog.